DATE DUE

THE LOST HORSE

塞翁失馬

近塞上之人。有善術者。馬無故亡而入胡。人皆弔之。其父曰。此何遽不為福乎。居數月。其馬將胡駿馬而歸。人皆賀之。其父曰。此何遽不能為禍乎。家富良馬。其子好騎。墮而折其髀。人皆弔之。其父曰。此何遽不為福乎。居一年。胡人大入塞。丁壯者引弦而戰。近塞之人。死者十九。此獨以跛之故。父子相保。

《淮南子・人間訓》

THE LOST HORSE

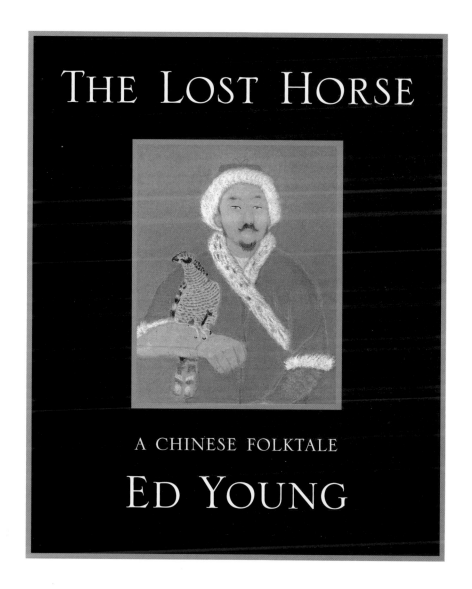

A CHINESE FOLKTALE

ED YOUNG

Voyager Books

Harcourt, Inc.

ORLANDO   AUSTIN   NEW YORK   SAN DIEGO   TORONTO   LONDON

IN NORTHERN CHINA there once lived a wise man called Sai

He had few possessions but owned
a horse that was both strong and fast.

One day a violent thunderstorm struck the land.
Terrified, the horse escaped into the night.

One by one the people came to comfort Sai for his loss.
"You know, it may not be such a bad thing,"
he told them.

To the people's surprise, the horse returned a few days later with a mare, equally fast and strong.

When the people came to congratulate Sai on his good fortune, he replied, "Perhaps it is not such a good thing."

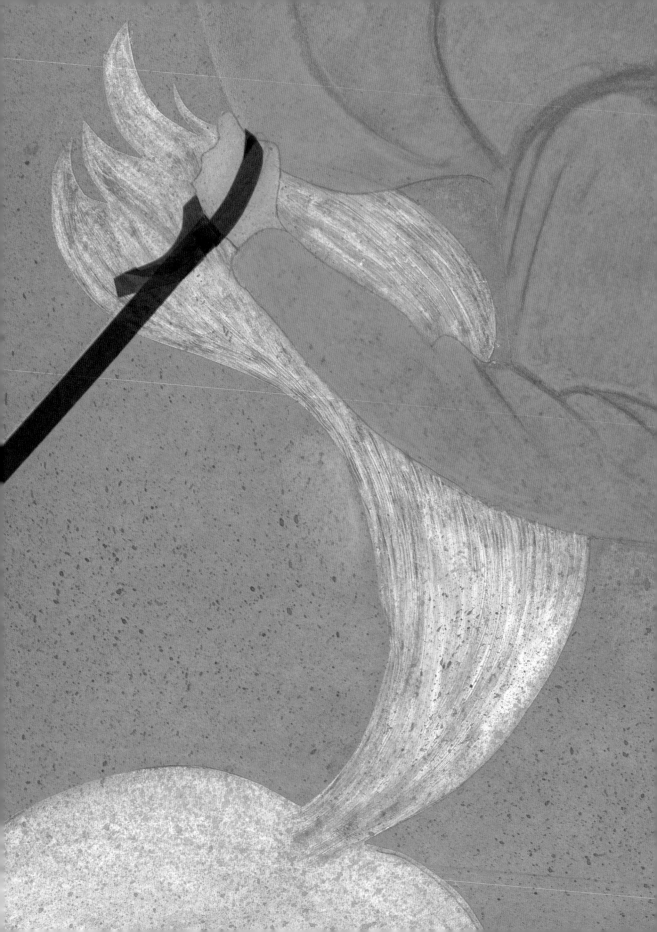

The next month Sai's son decided to take the mare for a ride. The horse threw him and he broke his leg.

When people came to console Sai, again he said,

"It could be this is not such a bad thing."

Later that year hostile nomads invaded China's northern border. All able-bodied men took up arms to defend their home.

Though peace followed, many did not return.
Because of his injury, Sai's son was spared.

Sai's son had learned from his father to
trust in the ever changing fortunes of life.
Together, for all the days that followed,
Sai and his son lived in harmony.

www.HarcourtBooks.com

First Voyager Books edition 2004
Voyager Books is a trademark of Harcourt, Inc.,
registered in the United States of America
and/or other jurisdictions.

The Library of Congress has cataloged the
hardcover edition as follows:
Young, Ed.
The lost horse/Ed Young.
p.   cm.
Summary: A retelling of the tale about a Chinese
man who owned a marvelous horse and who
believed that things were not always as bad,
or as good, as they might seem.
[1. Folklore—China.]   I. Title.
PZ8.1.Y84Lp   1998
398.2'0951'02—dc21
[E]   96-52861
ISBN 0-15-201061-5
ISBN 0-15-205023-X pb

H G F E D C B A

The illustrations in this book were done in collage
with pastel and watercolor.
The text type was set in Bembo.
The display type was set in Serlio.
Color separations by Tien Wah Press, Singapore
Printed and bound by Tien Wah Press, Singapore
Production supervision by Sandra Grebenar
and Wendi Taylor
Designed by Michael Farmer

ABOUT THIS BOOK

In China the story of The Lost Horse is a proverb with four characters.
The Chinese calligraphy beginning this book narrates the original Chinese
story, and my English text is adapted from that in a fuller telling for readers of
all ages. There are also variations of "The Lost Horse" that exist
throughout the Middle East.

ED YOUNG

ED YOUNG immigrated to the United States from China when he was twenty, and since then has written and illustrated several award-winning books for children, including the Caldecott Medal–winning *Lon Po Po: A Red-Riding Hood Story from China;* the Caldecott Honor book *Seven Blind Mice;* and *I Wish I Were a Butterfly,* written by James Howe. Ed Young's retelling of Chinese folktales is universally praised for combining graceful prose and elegant illustrations in a way that brings them to life for children of all ages. Mr. Young lives in New York.